Stardust

Night Shade

To Molly Tarris and Castaway, a very special horse,
who is cantering with the unicorns now – LC

To Jenny – LF

STRIPES PUBLISHING
An imprint of the Little Tiger Group
1 Coda Studios, 189 Munster Road,
London SW6 6AW

A paperback original
First published in Great Britain in 2018

Text copyright © Linda Chapman, 2018
Illustrations copyright © Lucy Fleming, 2018

ISBN: 978-1-84715-947-2

Printed and bound in the UK.

2 4 6 8 10 9 7 5 3 1

Star Friends

Night Shade

LINDA CHAPMAN
ILLUSTRATED BY LUCY FLEMING

IN THE STAR WORLD

Millions of tiny stars shone in the velvet-black sky, casting a sparkling light over the mountains and valleys, forests and lakes. In a wood, four of the wisest animals in the Star World had gathered around a forest pool – an owl, a wolf, a stag and a badger. Their fur and feathers glittered with stardust and their eyes were a deep indigo blue.

"How are the four young Star Animals who travelled to the human world to find Star Friends?" asked the badger.

"It must be three months now since they and their Star Friends stopped the old lady who was using dark magic," said the stag.

"Indeed it is." Hunter, the owl, touched the pool with the tip of his wing and the water shimmered. "And Westcombe is peaceful again." A picture appeared in the water. It showed a pretty Devon village with stone cottages, thatched roofs and narrow streets. "The person using dark magic has forgotten all about magic, and the Star Friends have been using the magic current to help people," Hunter said. "Every good deed they do strengthens the current."

"Can we see the animals and their Star Friends?" asked the wolf eagerly.

Hunter nodded and swept his wing across the pool. The picture changed, showing four girls and four animals running into a clearing in a wood. The girls were laughing and the animals – a fox, a squirrel, a deer and a wildcat – were bounding along beside them.

Behind the girls, a small waterfall splashed over grey rocks and flowed away in a stream that then ran through the trees down to the sea. It was early spring and the stream was swollen with rainwater.

"Maia, Ionie, Sita and Lottie," said the wolf softly, looking at each of the girls.

Maia, who had dark blond hair and a sideways fringe was chasing after the young fox, while Ionie was stepping into a patch of shadows with the wildcat beside her. They vanished and reappeared on the other side of the clearing. Sita, who had long dark hair and gentle brown eyes, spotted something in the grass and hurried over, with the deer trotting beside her. Crouching down, Sita picked up a baby bird that had fallen from its nest. She called to Lottie, who took the bird. Tucking it into a pocket of her coat, she swung herself into a tree and climbed up to the bird's nest with Juniper, the red squirrel, next to her.

"They look very happy," the badger said contentedly.

But as the animals watched, a dark cloud began to swirl across the image.

The stag pawed the ground. "What does this darkness mean, Hunter?"

The owl looked uneasy. "I think it is a warning to us that more evil is heading for Westcombe."

"So soon?" said the badger.

Hunter nodded. "The clearing is a crossing place between our world and the human world, which makes it an area of very powerful magic. People who want to use magic for evil purposes will always be attracted to it."

The wolf padded around the pool. "I wish we could help."

"We cannot," said Hunter, a sad look in his round eyes. "We have had our time in the human world. It is up to the young Star Animals and their Star Friends to defeat this new threat."

"But what is it?" questioned the stag.

"I do not know," said Hunter, staring at the water. "Let us watch and see…"

Chapter One

Maia touched Bracken's rusty red fur. "Got you!"

The fox cub gave an excited yap as Maia raced away. She could feel magic tingling through her. When she connected with the current that flowed between the human world and the Star World, as Bracken had taught her, she could do all sorts of amazing things – see into the past, get glimpses of the future and watch things that were happening elsewhere. Now, she used the magic to see where Bracken was going to move so she could dodge out of the way. She moved to the left, saw him start to jump that way and dodged right at the last second, but Bracken knew her tricks well. He turned in the air and hit her chest with his front paws, sending her toppling to the ground.

"Got you back, Maia!" Bracken said, snuffling at her hair. She rolled him over, tickling the pale, downy fur on his tummy. He squirmed in delight, his bushy tail waving from side to side.

Maia felt a rush of happiness. She loved being a Star Friend! It was amazing being able to do magic with her three best friends and their Star Animals. The girls all had different magical abilities. Lottie could use magic to be incredibly fast and agile; Ionie could travel to places using shadows, and make illusions appear; Sita could soothe and heal, and she also had the awesome ability to command anyone to do as she wanted – which thankfully she didn't use very often.

"Hey, guys!" Lottie called, sounded slightly anxious. "Come over here a moment." She jumped down from the tree.

"Did you put the baby bird back in the nest?" Maia said, going over with Bracken.

Lottie nodded. "It's fine but I noticed something strange while I was doing it." Her hazel eyes looked worried. Juniper leaped from the tree and landed lightly on her shoulder. His little paws played with the ends of her dark hair.

"What is it?" said Ionie, appearing in the patch of shadows beside Lottie, with Sorrel next to her.

"The trees don't have any green spring buds any more," Lottie said.

"That's weird," said Ionie. "There are leaf buds on the trees outside my bedroom window at home and there's even blossom on the cherry tree in our front garden. I wonder why there aren't any spring buds here yet?"

Juniper bobbed up and down on Lottie's shoulder, his red tail flicking around anxiously. "It's not that there aren't any *yet* but rather that the buds here are turning brown. They were green a week ago but now they're all withering."

Maia realized something else that was odd. "There are usually spring flowers here in February. I used to come here with my granny to pick daffodils and snowdrops."

"There *were* some snowdrops last week,"
said Sita. "I found a baby mouse near some."
She went to the edge of the clearing. "Yes!
Here!" She crouched down and then looked
back over her shoulder in confusion. "They've
died."

The others hurried over. The snowdrops by
Sita's feet had shrivelled up.

"This isn't good," said Sorrel, stalking
around the brown clump of withered

snowdrops, her whiskers quivering. "Trees and plants don't just die in early spring. I suspect dark magic must be going on here."

"Do you think it's someone conjuring Shades?" Sita said uneasily.

Shades were evil spirits who lived in the Shadow World. They could be conjured from the shadows by dark magic and then trapped in everyday objects. When those objects were placed in people's homes, the Shades began to cause misery and chaos. As Star Friends it was the girls' job to work with their Star Animals to send Shades back to their own world. So far the girls had fought a Mirror Shade who had been making Maia's older sister extremely jealous of her best friend; a Wish Shade who had made wishes come true in horrible ways; and four Fear Shades trapped in little yellow stretchy men who had terrified people.

"If someone is conjuring Shades, we'll stop them," said Ionie determinedly.

A sharp thrill ran through Maia. Although fighting Shades was dangerous it was also very exciting.

"Your bravery is admirable," Sorrel told Ionie. "However, I cannot smell any Shades here."

"Neither can I," said Willow, her delicate nostrils flaring. Some Star Animals like Sorrel and Willow had a particular talent for smelling if Shades were near.

"So what's going on?" said Lottie, looking round.

"Remember, dark magic isn't just used for conjuring Shades," said Juniper.

"Yes, Auntie Mabel used it to make that horrible snow globe," said Maia, stroking Bracken and thinking of the old lady who had been using dark magic. She'd trapped Bracken and Willow inside a crystal globe. Maia would never forget how she had felt when she thought she would never see Bracken again.

It had been the worst moment of her life.

"Indeed. You girls use the current of Star Magic when you do magic but some people use the magic contained inside crystals or plants," Sorrel said. "Many people who use plants do good but others perform very powerful dark magic by pulling the life force from plants and trees, leaving them dying." Sorrel touched the dead snowdrops with her nose. "It could explain what is happening in this clearing."

"How can we find out if that's what's going on?" Maia said.

Bracken put his paws up on her knees. "You could use your magic to see if anything strange has happened here in the last week."

"Go on, Maia," Ionie urged.

Maia sat down on a tree stump. Pulling a small mirror out of her coat pocket, she looked into it. She needed a shiny surface if she wanted to use magic to see into the past or future. Cupping it in her hands, she let her mind open up to the current. Magic swirled into her, sparkling and tingling through her veins. "Show me if someone has been using dark magic here in the clearing," she said.

The surface of the mirror misted over for a moment and then a picture formed. Maia was the only one who could see it and so she described it out loud. "I'm seeing the clearing at night-time," she said. "Someone's coming into the clearing. They're wearing a long dark coat with a hood. It's a woman, I think." The figure in the mirror looked around and then hurried to the centre of the clearing, where she used liquid from a small bottle to mark a circle on the ground around herself. The circle lit up with a faint green light. The person corked the bottle and then put a silver bowl down in the centre of the circle. She straightened up, showing a glimpse of blond hair.

"She's drawn a circle around herself with

some kind of potion," said Maia. "And now she's putting leaves into a metal bowl." She saw the woman wave her hand over the bowl and mutter some words. "It's like she's doing some sort of spell…" She gasped as the woman threw her arms in the air. The branches of the trees appeared to be pulled towards her as if by an invisible force. Wind whipped around the clearing, tossing her coat about her legs. The woman clasped her fingers together and leaves suddenly exploded off the trees, flying high into the sky. The wind stopped and the trees' branches sagged, the buds shrivelling. Around the woman, the leaves floated slowly to the ground like sad confetti.

"What can you see?" Ionie asked impatiently.

Maia quickly told them. "Now she's picking up the bowl. The leaves have changed into a liquid. It's dark – almost black." She watched as the woman poured it into an empty bottle she took from her pocket, then she stepped outside the circle. The light vanished and she hurried away. "She's gone," Maia said slowly.

Sorrel hissed. "It seems someone has been doing dark magic here just as I suspected."

"But what for?" said Willow.

"And who is this woman?" said Bracken.

"I'll see if the magic will show me," said Maia. She looked into her mirror again. "Show me the face of the person doing dark magic," she said hopefully.

The hooded figure appeared in the mirror again but her face was a blur. Maia shook her head. "She must be using a blocking spell to hide herself from anyone spying on her."

"We need to find out who she is," said Lottie.

"And stop her!" declared Ionie.

Just then, Maia's phone rang, making them all jump. She checked the screen. "It's my mum."

"Where are you all?" her mum asked as she answered. "If you want to go to that new shop in town before the film, we need to leave Westcombe in five minutes."

"Sorry, Mum. We lost track of time. We're in the woods by Granny Anne's cottage," Maia said.

"I'll drive to the top of the lane," said her mum. "Meet me there in five."

"OK." Maia clicked the phone off. "Mum says we need to go now."

The four girls had arranged a trip to the movies for the last afternoon of their February half-term holiday.

"We'd better go and meet Mum," Maia told Bracken. "But I promise we'll try to find out who's doing dark magic here."

Bracken licked Maia's nose and then he and the other animals disappeared in a swirl of starry light. They could vanish in an instant but would always reappear again when the girls called their names.

The Star Friends took one last look around the clearing with its bare-branched trees and and then hurried away down the overgrown footpath.

CHAPTER TWO

The footpath came out on a little stony lane.
To the right, the lane led down to the cliffs
and sea, and to the left, it led back up to the
main road and village. Opposite the entrance
to the footpath was a thatched cottage with
a pretty garden and a little white front gate.
Maia's heart twisted as she looked at it. It had
been her granny's home before she died but
now it had new owners.

The new family hadn't moved in straight
away. Painters and decorators had come and

gone and a conservatory had been quickly built on to the back. However, a few days ago, the removal lorries had turned up. Now, a white van was parked outside the cottage and a tall, slim woman, about Maia's mum's age, was directing two men as they carried some giant pot plants inside.

The lady smiled in greeting. "Hi, Maia!"

"Hi!" Maia called back. She had met the lady – Esther – with her mum when she had come to look round the cottage. "Is the move going OK?"

"Yes, thank you. We're just about done. Can you tell your mum I'll call in and have a coffee with her soon?" Esther said.

"I will! Bye!" Maia hurried after her friends.

"She seems nice," Sita said.

"Yes. She and Mum went to school together." Maia glanced at Lottie. "Your mum was with them, too."

Lottie nodded. "Mum said she knew her but they weren't really good friends."

"She's got a daughter, hasn't she?" Ionie said to Maia.

"Yes, I haven't met her but she's starting at our school tomorrow. I think she's in Year Six like us."

"We'll have to help her settle in," said Sita. "I'd hate to start a new school in the middle of Year Six."

Mrs Greene – Maia's mum – was waiting at the top of the lane in her car with the engine running. "Honestly, you girls," she said as they scrambled into the car. "We'd better get a move on or we won't get a chance to go to *Fairytales*."

"My sister, Simi, went on the first day it opened," said Sita. "She says they've got all sorts of amazing stuff – models of fairies, elves and unicorns, cards that can tell the future, jewellery, posters and books."

"It sounds awesome." Maia remembered something. "Oh, Mum, we just saw Esther. She said to say hi and that she'd call in for a coffee soon."

"OK, great – it'll be good to have a proper catch-up." Mrs Greene shook her head. "It's funny how you can spend every day with people at school when you're younger but then you all go your separate ways. I'd heard Esther had started a business making herbal face creams and body lotions but I didn't even know she'd got married and had a child until she came to look round the cottage."

Maia frowned, thinking that there was no

way she would ever lose touch with Lottie, Sita and Maia. "Why didn't you stay friends?"

Her mum shrugged. "We were in different friendship groups at school. Esther was one of the popular girls. My friends were more into reading and studying."

Maia grinned. "So you were a geek, Mum!"

"There's nothing wrong with being a geek," Ionie said.

"Nope. Geeks rule!" said Lottie. They high-fived each other. Both of them were very clever and always did very well in tests and exams.

"Well said, girls," said Mrs Greene approvingly. "Now, you'll all help Esther's daughter, Essie, settle in, won't you?"

"Of course we will," Maia said.

"She'll either be with Maia and Ionie in Miss Harris's class or in Mr Neal's class with me and Lottie," Sita said. "So we'll be able to make sure she's OK."

Mrs Greene smiled and drove on. When they got to town, they parked near the new shop. It was tucked away down a little street with a cobbled alleyway on one side. It had a wooden sign with gold writing saying *Fairytales,* an old-fashioned front window and a bell that rang as they walked inside. The air smelled of incense, and the wind chimes that hung from the ceiling were tinkling gently. The shelves were filled with fantasy figures and colourful packets of herbs.

A lady in her fifties with shoulder-length blond hair was standing behind the counter. "Welcome to *Fairytales.*" She beamed. "I'm Alice. Let me know if I can help you."

"Thank you," Maia's mum said. "The girls have been longing to come in to have a look around."

"Come in, dearies," Alice said.

"Oh, wow," said Sita, heading over to a shelf with unicorn models. "Look at these."

"Aren't these sweet, too?" said Lottie, picking up a stone egg that had a dragon hatching out.

"Look with your eyes not with your hands," Alice trilled.

Lottie glanced at Maia. How old did Alice

think they were?

Maia's mum browsed some leaflets while the girls looked around. "Oh, the Westcombe beachcomber sculpture competition," she said to Alice as she picked up a flyer. "We live in Westcombe and it's always such a big thing. Lots of people enter – my next-door neighbour always makes something incredible and usually wins."

"I'm entering this year. I love collecting things from the beach and making things," said Alice. She winked at Maia. "And maybe the fairies at the bottom of my garden will give me a helping hand!"

Maia smiled politely and escaped to join Ionie, who was looking at a display of friendship bracelets with silver charms on. "I like these – and look at those dreamcatchers." Ionie pointed at the wall where some brightly coloured turquoise, purple and pink dreamcatchers were hanging. They were made

with feathers and
ribbon stitched
on to a hoop.
"They're
beautiful."

"Hang one
at the end of
your bed and
they'll catch any
bad dreams as you
sleep," Alice called.

"How much are
they?" Ionie asked.

"Eight pounds each," said
Alice. "But there are plenty of other cheaper
things." She pointed to the shelf beneath the
dreamcatchers. "There are some sleep-easy
herbs and oils, or you could get a crystal.
Crystals like rose quartz can bring good
dreams, too."

Maia felt a chill run down her spine as she

looked at the crystals on display. Auntie Mabel
had used crystals to do dark magic.

"I don't think we'll buy a crystal," she said
quickly. "Maybe a bracelet though."

She got out her purse and bought a bracelet.
Ionie got one, too. Lottie bought a dragon
egg and Sita bought a unicorn, although she
couldn't choose between them so in the end
Lottie chose for her – Sita was hopeless at
making decisions.

"Right, come on, girls," said Mrs Greene,
checking her watch. "We really have to go."

"How was the movie?" Maia's dad asked when
Maia and her mum got home. He was in
the kitchen making supper with Clio, Maia's
fifteen-year-old sister. Alfie, their little brother,
was playing with his trains on the table.

"It was good," Maia said. It had been a
funny film about animals on a rescue mission

but she had found it hard to concentrate because she kept thinking about the clearing. She really wanted to talk to Bracken and she headed for the door.

"Wait a mo. Before you go, I saw this today." Mr Greene held up a flyer. "There's a quiz at the village hall in a couple of weeks. I think we should enter as a family."

Clio groaned. "A quiz? Do we have to, Dad?"

Her dad nodded. "It'll be fun to do something together. We might lose horribly but who cares?"

"I think it's a great idea," agreed Mrs Greene.

"If we're going to do something as a family can't we just go to The Copper Kettle?" Maia said. It was the café in the village and she loved going there for a treat – the cakes were delicious!

"I think we should do something where we use our brains," her dad said. "It will be good for us!" He beamed.

Just then Maia's mum's phone pinged. She

checked it and sighed. "Ellie and Jo want to go for a run tonight. I suppose I'd better find my trainers, although I'd rather have a cup of tea." She'd recently taken up running because she and her friends were entering a charity fun run but she really didn't like it.

Maia slipped away to her bedroom.

"Bracken!" she whispered as she shut the door firmly behind her.

Bracken appeared in a haze of silver light and put his paws on her knees, his dark eyes shining with happiness at seeing her. "Have you had a good time?"

"It was OK," Maia said, stroking him. "But I couldn't concentrate. I kept thinking about the clearing and the woman who I saw doing dark magic there."

"I know," he said. "I wish we could find out who she is."

"I thought I might use my magic to see what is going to happen," said Maia. She'd been thinking about it at the cinema. Her magic could give her a glimpse of the future and might help them work out what was going on.

"Try! Go on!" urged Bracken.

Maia sat down at her desk and looked into the mirror there. "Show me what's coming," she whispered.

The surface swirled and then pictures began to flash across it: a hooded figure crouching down in the clearing at dusk... A wicker basket filled with plants... A collection of small bottles filled with dark liquids... A shelf covered with crystals with a blur of bright colours behind them...

The images faded.

"What did you see?" Bracken asked.

Maia frowned and described the pictures she'd seen.

"You saw plants *and* crystals?" Bracken said, his ears pricking. "Maybe the person doing dark magic is using crystal magic as well as plant magic."

"Mmm." There was something about
the image of the shelf with crystals that was
nagging at Maia. It had seemed very familiar.
Crystals… Crystals…

Suddenly she gasped. "The crystals. They
had dreamcatchers hanging behind them.
They're in a shop called *Fairytales* in town!"

"A shop?" Bracken echoed.

"Yes, it's only been open a week."

Bracken bounced around. "A week? Maia,
that's about when the clearing started to
change. This could be a clue."

Maia stared at him. "The woman in there did seem odd. Maybe she's the person doing dark magic. I've got to tell the others!"

She pulled her phone out of her pocket and texted Ionie, Sita and Lottie. She longed to tell them everything but she knew she couldn't risk explaining in a text in case their parents checked their phones.

Need to talk to u all. Meet b4 schl 2moro. I've seen something that might be VERY important! Don't be late! Mxx

She pressed 'send'.

"Done," she said to Bracken. "I'll talk to them tomorrow and then we can all meet after school and work out what to do." She hugged him tightly. "I hope this helps us find out what's going on!"

Chapter Three

"What's up?" Lottie demanded the next morning. The four girls had run to a quiet corner of the playground where they could talk without being overheard. "I could hardly sleep last night. What's so important, Maia?"

"Yes, tell us!" Ionie demanded.

Maia quickly explained about the shelf of crystals from *Fairytales*. "Maybe the person doing dark magic is using crystals as well as plant magic."

"And maybe it's Alice!" breathed Ionie.

"I thought she seemed quite nice," said Sita, looking troubled.

"We all thought Auntie Mabel was nice but she was doing dark magic and trying to hurt us," Ionie reminded her.

"Alice could be just as bad as Auntie Mabel," said Maia, excitement swirling in her tummy. "We need to find out more about her."

"Should we all meet after school?" Ionie said.

"Yes. At mine," said Maia.

"I'll only be able to stay until five," said Lottie. "I've got gymnastics but I'll ask if I can come until then." Lottie and her sister did lots of activities and she found it harder than the others to meet up after school.

"Maia!" Maia heard her mum call. "I'm going now."

Maia ran over to say goodbye. As she did so, she saw a new girl coming into the playground. She was very pretty, her blond hair was in a high ponytail and she had lip gloss on. She was with a tall man with a bushy black beard.

"Do you think that's Essie?" Maia whispered to her mum.

Her mum did a double take. "It has to be," she said. "She's the image of Esther when she was younger."

She went over to the man and girl. "Hi, I'm Nicky Greene and this is my daughter, Maia."

Essie beamed. "Oh, hi. Mum said to look out for you and Maia." She glanced at her dad who hadn't said a word. "Say hi, Dad."

He nodded. His eyes were a very bright green. "Hello," he muttered into his beard. He seemed a bit odd.

"You can go home if you want, Dad," said Essie, giving him a little push. "I'll be fine." She looked at Maia. "You'll show me what to do, won't you, Maia?"

"Yes, sure," said Maia.

Essie's dad walked away. Maia stared after him. Weird! He hadn't even said goodbye!

"How are you feeling about starting here, Essie?" Mrs Greene asked. "I imagine Westcombe Primary will be quite different from your school in London."

"It's a lot smaller," said Essie. She flicked her hair confidently over her shoulder as she looked around. "But I don't mind starting a new school. I'm sure I'm going to have fun!"

Maia introduced Essie to Ionie, Lottie and Sita. As Essie glanced over them, Maia saw her friends as they must appear to the new girl: Ionie neat and tidy as always, her uniform and shoes sensible rather than fashionable, her strawberry-blond hair tied back in a ponytail.

Lottie loved clothes and was wearing a pretty red cardigan with her grey school skirt and shiny patent shoes. Her dark curls were clipped back with a red slide. Sita, on the other hand, wasn't into fashion at all and happily wore her sister's old school uniform. Maia wasn't sure if she imagined it but she thought she saw a faint sneer on Essie's face as she took in Sita's faded sweatshirt and grey trousers with paint stains on.

"Do you know which class you're in?" Ionie asked her.

"My teacher is Mr Neal," said Essie.

"That means you'll be with me and Lottie," said Sita. "We'll look after you."

"Thanks," Essie said. She turned to Lottie and gave her a bright smile. "I like your bag."

Lottie smiled back. "I like yours, too." Essie had a black bag covered with red hearts. "And your shoes."

Essie put one foot next to Lottie's. "They're very like yours, aren't they? Hey, do you want to swap phone numbers?" She pulled a shiny iPhone out of her pocket.

"Nice phone," said Lottie.

"Mum always gets me the latest model," said Essie airily.

"Well, if you don't want it confiscated, you'd better put it away," Ionie said quite sharply. Maia glanced at her. Ionie had no time for people who were into fashion and phones and stuff like that.

Essie looked surprised. "Really? Why?"

"We're not allowed phones at school. If the teachers see it they'll take it off you," Maia explained. "Did your old school let you have them?"

"They did," Essie said slowly, "but I can see it's going to be different here." She put her phone into her bag. "It's going to take me a while to get used to the new rules."

Just then the bell rang.

"Come on, Sita and I will show you where to line up," Lottie said.

"OK. See you later, Maia," Essie said.

"See you!" Maia called, noticing that Essie hadn't said goodbye to Ionie. From the way Ionie's expression had tightened it was clear she had noticed, too.

At breaktime, Essie and Lottie came out of their classroom together with Sita following behind them.

"How's it going?" Maia asked Essie.

"Great, thanks." Essie linked her arm through Lottie's. "Lottie's been so helpful."

"Mr Neal's asked me to be Essie's buddy," Lottie said.

"We're sitting next to each other," Essie said. "And we're doing a project on volcanoes together. We've got some brilliant ideas for it already. Lottie's really clever," she said to the others.

Lottie looked pleased.

Maia glanced at Sita. She was being very quiet. "Who are you doing a project with?" she asked her. Sita usually worked with Lottie.

"Jack," said Sita.

Maia gave her a sympathetic look. Jack was loud and messed around.

"I think Jack likes Essie," Lottie said with a grin. "Tyler, too. They keep coming over and asking her if she needs anything."

Essie giggled. "They're both quite cute." She looked at Maia, Ionie and Sita. "Have you got boyfriends?"

"No," said Sita.

Ionie rolled her eyes. "Please tell me you're not one of those dumb girls who just want to talk about boys, are you?"

Maia saw Essie's eyes narrow and felt a distinct chill fall.

"So what do you like doing, Essie?" she said quickly.

"Shopping and hanging out with friends," Essie said, turning her back on Ionie. "I like inventing dances and watching YouTube videos about make-up."

"That sounds cool," Maia said, catching sight

of Ionie rolling her eyes.

Essie smiled at her. "You'll have to come round to my house. You, too, Lottie. Oh, look," she said suddenly. "Tara and Sadie are waving. I'm going to go and say hi. Catch you back in class, Lottie. Bye, Maia." She went over to where Tara and Sadie were. They were two of the prettiest and most popular girls in Year Six.

"I don't like her," Ionie said decisively.

"You've only just met her," Maia said, although she did kind of agree with Ionie. She didn't like the way Essie had ignored Ionie and Sita as she walked off.

"We should give her a chance," said Sita. "She may turn out to be nice."

Maia saw Ionie open her mouth to argue. "Look, let's not waste breaktime talking about Essie," she said hastily. "We've got fr more important things to discuss."

To her relief, the others nodded and they headed off for their favourite quiet place in the playground. There was a grassy bank and a low wall to sit on.

"Have you thought about what I said this morning?" Maia whispered.

"I can't stop thinking about it," said Ionie. "I think we should go to *Fairytales* after school and see if we can find out anything more."

"But how will we get into town?" Maia said.

Ionie grinned and pushed back her strawberry-blond ponytail. "With magic, of course!"

Chapter Four

When school finished, the four girls hurried
back to Maia's house. As they arrived, they
heard the sound of crying. Alfie was sitting on
Clio's knee in the kitchen. There were tears
running down his face.

"What's happened?" Maia asked.

Clio sighed. "Mum asked me to babysit
while she went for a run, and Alfie decided to
see if Mr Rabbit could fly. He threw him out
of his bedroom window and now he's stuck in
the tree outside the window!"

"Oh, Alfie!" Maia groaned. Mr Rabbit was Alfie's favourite cuddly toy. He couldn't sleep without him.

"Want Mr Rabbit!" Alfie's voice rose in a wail.

"It's OK, Alfie. Dad will get a ladder and get him down from the tree when he comes home," said Clio, stroking her brother's hair.

"Want him now!" Alfie sobbed.

Maia glanced at Lottie. Could she help?

Lottie saw the look. "Let me see what I can do," she said. "I'm good at climbing."

"There's no way you can climb all the way up into the branches where he is," said Clio.

But Lottie was already heading out of the French doors that led into the back garden.

Sita crouched down, taking Alfie's hands.

"Shh, Alfie, shh," she soothed. "It's going to be OK. You're going to get Mr Rabbit back. Don't cry any more."

Alfie's sobs dried to hiccups. Maia knew that Sita was using her calming powers. Alfie stared at Sita, his blue eyes wide. "Mr Rabbit come back?" he said.

"Yes," she said.

He smiled.

"Here he is!" Lottie said rather breathlessly, appearing in the doorway a few minutes later with Alfie's cuddly rabbit in her hand.

Clio gaped. "How did you get him?"

Lottie grinned. "I told you. I'm good at climbing." She kicked off her shoes and brought Mr Rabbit over to Alfie. Alfie grabbed him and hugged him as if he was never going to let him go.

Maia smiled. She loved it when they were able to use magic to help solve little everyday problems and make people happier. She grabbed a packet of chocolate biscuits. "Let's go to my room."

They hurried upstairs.

"Thanks for getting Alfie's rabbit," Maia said to Lottie as she shut her bedroom door.

"No probs. It was fun!" said Lottie. "You can see all sorts of stuff if you climb up trees. I saw your neighbour making a giant swan out of driftwood. He didn't see me though."

"It must be for that beachcomber sculpture competition," said Maia. "He always wins." She opened the biscuits and handed them out. "Now, let's get on with some more magic!"

They called the animals who appeared and bounded around them in delight.

"Maia!" Bracken said, leaping into her arms and licking her neck. She hugged him tightly and buried her face in his soft fur. She missed him so much when she was at school. Next to her, her friends were greeting their animals with cuddles, too.

They all settled down and the girls told the animals of the plan they had come up with. They had decided that Ionie and Maia would shadow-travel to *Fairytales*. They would take Sorrel with them and see if she could smell any Shades. Lottie and Sita were going to stay behind in Maia's room – Lottie had to be there in case her mum arrived early to take her to gymnastics and Sita said she was happy to stay and make an excuse if Maia's mum came looking for them.

"I wish I could come with you," Bracken said, sighing.

"I know, but people might wonder what was going on if wild animals like you or Willow or Juniper turned up in a shop," she said.

"How will you take Sorrel inside?" said Willow. "People don't normally walk into shops with cats, do they?"

Maia grinned at Ionie. "No, but we have an idea for that, too!"

Ten minutes later, Ionie was holding a plastic pet carrier that Maia had brought in from the garage. Sorrel was inside it, the tip of her tabby tail quivering furiously. "I cannot believe I am doing this!" she hissed. "Imprisoned in a cage like a common house cat!"

"Sorrel, we've been through this," Ionie soothed. "You just need to pretend to be a normal cat so we can get you into the shop in this crate."

"And you're not really imprisoned," Maia

pointed out. "You could magic yourself out of there at any moment."

Bracken pressed his nose against the wire-mesh door. "Be a good little pussycat, Sorrel," he teased.

Sorrel swiped a paw at him, her claws clanging against the wire mesh. "Watch it, Fox!" she spat.

Bracken yapped as if he was laughing.

Ionie glanced at Maia. "I think we'd better go!"

They stepped into the shadow of Maia's wardrobe and the world spun away. Just a few seconds later, Maia's feet met solid ground and she realized they were standing in the shadows of the alleyway next to *Fairytales*. Luckily no one was there to witness their sudden arrival.

"Time to see what we can find out," said

Ionie, her green eyes sparkling.

The girls pushed the door to *Fairytales* open.

"Hello again, dearies," said Alice. She was putting out some new dreamcatchers behind the shelf of crystals.

"Do you mind if we bring my cat in?" said Ionie. "We're just on the way to the vet but we really wanted to come and have another look around."

Alice beamed. "No problem at all. I love animals."

The girls shut the door and Alice put down the dreamcatchers and came over. "Who's a little cutie-pie?" she cooed to Sorrel in a high-pitched voice. "Who's a precious kittycat?"

Sorrel hissed.

"Oh dearie me. Someone isn't in a very good mood," said Alice. "Does the pussycat not like going to the nasty vet's?"

"No, she doesn't," said Ionie hastily as Sorrel spat. "I'll just put her down here."

She placed the carrier on the floor near the shelf with crystals.

"So what can I help you with today?" said Alice. "If you want a dreamcatcher, you'd better buy one fast. They're selling like hot cakes at the moment!"

"I just want to look at the bracelets again," Ionie said. She and Maia pretended to examine the bracelets, glancing at Sorrel to see if she was showing any signs that she could smell Shades, but she had retreated to the back of the carrier and all they could see was the tip of her tail.

Maia looked all around the rest of the shop, but there was nothing to suggest Alice was performing dark magic.

After five minutes, Ionie bought another bracelet so that Alice wouldn't think it was strange they were calling in without buying anything. Then they left and hurried back into the alleyway.

"Well, did you smell any Shades in the

shop?" Ionie asked Sorrel.

"No, I didn't, but I did feel magic in the air." Sorrel pressed her face to the mesh. "Now, let me out of here!"

"As soon as we're back home," Ionie promised, grabbing Maia's hand and stepping into the shadows.

When Maia, Ionie and Sorrel got back to Maia's bedroom they let Sorrel out straight away.

"Did you learn anything?" said Lottie.

"I learned I do not like that woman who owns the shop." Sorrel bristled. "Kittycat indeed!" she huffed.

Bracken and Juniper sniggered and Sorrel glared at them.

"Stop it!" Willow told them. She blinked her large eyes at Sorrel. "It was very good of you, Sorrel, to put up with being in a cage just so we could find out more."

Sorrel looked slightly appeased.

"Did you smell any Shades there?" Sita asked.

Sorrel shook her head. "No. But I did sense magic in the shop."

"Dark magic?" said Maia.

"Just magic," Sorrel said, sitting down and wrapping her tail around her paws. "Our fur tingles when we are near magical objects or in places where magic is being used."

"So there was a feeling of magic but Alice doesn't seem to be conjuring Shades," said Maia thoughtfully. "She's got to be doing something with the crystals though, or why would the magic have shown them to me?" She rubbed her forehead. It was very confusing.

A knock on the bedroom door made them all jump. The animals vanished instantly.

Mrs Greene stuck her head round the door. "Lottie, your mum's here."

Maia went downstairs with Lottie to say goodbye. Mrs Thompson, Lottie's mum, was waiting in the hall.

"So how are things, Anna?" Maia's mum said.

"Very busy," Mrs Thompson replied as Lottie put her shoes on. "I'm completely rushed off my feet."

"I don't know how you manage to work and fit in all the after-school activities," said Mrs Greene. "Your girls do so many things. How do you do it?"

"With difficulty at times, but it's about looking to the future," Lottie's mum said. "If they want to go to a top university then all the extras will help. It's a competitive world out there, Nicky."

Mrs Greene laughed. "Oh, Anna. I can't believe you're thinking about university already. We've only just decided which secondary school Maia's going to!"

Just then there was a knock at the door.

"It's all go tonight," said Maia's mum, opening it. "Esther!" she said in surprise, seeing Essie's mum on the doorstep.

"Hi. Is now a good time to have that cup of coffee?" said Esther. She did a double take. "Anna. Gosh, I haven't seen you for years."

"I know. It must be twenty-five years," said Lottie's mum. "I heard you were moving back here. We'll have to catch up but not now. Lottie's got gymnastics."

"Another time then," said Esther.

Esther watched as Lottie and her mum got into Lottie's mum's smart white sports car. "Anna looks like she's done well for herself," she commented.

"She's an accountant for a soft drinks company," said Maia's mum.

"She was quiet as a mouse at school," said Esther, a strange note in her voice. "I'd never have guessed she'd go on to be so successful.

Sarah too – I heard she's a doctor."

"Sadie's mum?" said Mrs Greene. "Yes, she's a consultant at the hospital."

Esther shook her head and turned to Maia. "Essie said you and Lottie were really friendly today. Thank you."

"No problem," Maia said.

"She's going to have a few people round tomorrow after school for takeaway pizza and a movie – and she wants to ask you," Esther said. She looked at Mrs Greene a bit apologetically. "I know it's a school night but Essie really wants to make friends. Are you free, Maia?"

Maia hesitated. She actually wanted to meet with Ionie, Sita and Lottie after school. They needed to find out more

about Alice and the crystals. But her mum
answered for her.

"That'd be lovely, wouldn't it, Maia?"

"Yes. Thanks for inviting me," Maia said
politely and then, leaving the mums to chat,
she went upstairs to join the others.

Ionie and Sita were cuddling Willow and
Juniper. Bracken bounded over to Maia as she
shut the door. "We've been trying to work out
what to do next," he said.

"Did you have any ideas?" said Maia
hopefully.

"We think we should go to the clearing and
see if we can find any clues," said Ionie. "And
use magic to spy on Alice. How about we meet
at my house tomorrow?"

"Can't." Maia sighed. She told them about
the invite to Essie's. "She'll probably invite
you two as well."

"I don't think she'll invite me," said Ionie.

"Or me," said Sita. "I get the feeling she doesn't like me much. I don't know why. I've tried to be friendly."

"I wouldn't worry," said Ionie. "I think she only likes people who want to talk about boys and who don't have any brain cells."

"Thanks," Maia said, raising her eyebrows.

Ionie grinned. "I didn't mean you or Lottie, of course."

"So let's meet on Wednesday after school and go to the clearing then," Maia said.

Ionie nodded. "In the meantime we can watch out for anything odd. If dark magic is being used then bad things will soon start to happen."

Sita looked worried. "I hate the thought of Shades coming to Westcombe again and the plants in the clearing dying."

Maia nodded. "Don't worry, we'll soon work out what's going on – and stop it!"

CHAPTER FIVE

"So this is the kitchen and this is the lounge…" Essie gave a guided tour of her house the next day after school. As Ionie had predicted, Essie had not invited her or Sita to come along, just Lottie, Maia, Tara and Sadie. Both Essie's parents were out. "They often leave me on my own," Essie said airily. "I don't mind though."

Maia exchanged surprised looks with Lottie. Their parents never left them home alone. Even Clio wasn't left for long. Maia followed the others. It was really odd being in her granny's old house when it looked so different. The cosy clutter, flowery curtains and old rugs had been replaced by white walls and wooden floors, slatted blinds and smart leather chairs. There was a new conservatory filled with lush plants and wicker furniture. And Esther's office – once Granny Anne's dining room – was filled with shelves with different pots and tubes of face and body cream, soap and bath oil.

Essie's black cat lay on one of the chairs in the lounge watching them.

Maia went to stroke it but it unsheathed its claws and glared at her in much the same way that Sorrel had glared at Alice. Maia hastily decided to leave it alone.

Upstairs, the four small bedrooms had been transformed into two large bedrooms. Essie's room had a double bed with a dark purple throw over the end and matching cushions, a white rug on the pale wooden floor, and sleek

white furniture. There was a computer on the
desk and a TV attached to the wall as well as an
en-suite bathroom.

"Lucky! I can't believe you've got a TV in
your room," Tara said.

"I wish my bedroom was like this," said
Sadie.

"It's perfect," said Lottie, looking around in
awe. "You're so lucky."

Essie looked smug. She opened a cupboard and showed off an entire shelf of make-up and nail polishes, all in neat rows. "This is my make-up studio. We'll do each other's make-up later and then I'll order a pizza for tea."

"You're allowed to order takeaways?" said Sadie.

Essie nodded. "Whenever I want."

Maia glanced at Lottie again. Essie seemed so grown up. She noticed a purple dreamcatcher hanging in the window and went over to have a look at it.

"Did you get this from *Fairytales?*" Maia asked Essie.

Essie nodded. "My mum bought it for me yesterday. It's nice, isn't it?"

"It's really pretty," said Sadie. "I wish I had one."

"Me, too," said Tara.

Essie smiled. "Well, luckily for you, I like to share things with my friends." She hurried out and came back with four dreamcatchers still in their plastic wrappers. "Here, you can have one each."

"Really?" said Lottie.

Essie nodded and handed them out. She gave pink and turquoise ones to Maia, Lottie and Sadie and a purple and red one to Tara.

"Why do you have so many of them?" Tara asked.

"Mum likes to buy things that she can use as birthday presents," Essie said airily. "She keeps them all in a big box in her room. But she won't mind me giving these to you. She's great like that."

"Wow, thanks!" said Sadie.

Essie beamed. "Now, shall we do our nails? I'll be the nail artist. You can choose whatever you want."

They sat down in a circle and Essie put some music on and began doing their nails. She was very good at it – she didn't smudge any of the nail varnish or leave any blobs of it on their skin but Maia found it quite dull. Essie had some old Enid Blyton books on her shelf that looked like they had probably belonged to her mum. Maia picked up a *Famous Five* book and started to read it while the others talked about make-up and the boys in class and the YouTubers they liked. Maia tuned out their voices and let the story pull her in.

Suddenly a hand slapped down on the book, knocking it out of her hands. Maia jumped. Essie was standing in front of her. "Don't be boring, Maia!"

Maia felt her temper prickle at Essie's bossy tone and the way she'd just knocked the book out of her hand but she guessed she had been a bit rude, reading and not joining in, and so she forced herself to smile. "Sorry."

"You're here to have fun, not to read," Essie said, picking up the book and throwing it to her. "You can borrow this if you want but don't read it now."

Maia caught it and put it in her bag, feeling irritated but trying not to say anything.

Essie smiled round at them all. "I think at school tomorrow we should have matching ponytails and hairslides." She pulled out a box of different hairslides. "I've got plenty of red ones. Let's style the ponytails now and put the slides in. I'll do yours, Maia."

Maia reluctantly let Essie brush her hair into a high ponytail. "It's got to be high," Essie told the others, pulling Maia's hair tightly as she held it above her head and twisted a band around it. "Low ponytails look so babyish."

"What, you mean like Sita's?" said Tara with a snigger.

Maia stiffened.

"Yeah. She should look in the mirror

sometimes." Essie laughed. "And have you seen how old her jumper is?"

"Her clothes are dodgy," Sadie agreed.

Maia jumped to her feet, pulling away from Essie. "Stop being mean! Sita's our friend." She looked at Lottie, who nodded.

"Sita's really nice," Lottie said.

"So stop being horrible!" Maia said, glaring round.

Essie shrugged. "Chill. But if you're in *my* squad you have to have a high ponytail!" She walked over and clipped a slide into Maia's hair, pushing it extra hard against her scalp and making Maia wince. "OK, Lottie," she said brightly. "Let me do your hair, then when we've all got ponytails, I'll order the pizza and we can watch a movie."

"Awesome!" said Sadie.

Lottie went over so Essie could do her hair. Maia folded her arms and sat down on the bed, wishing she was somewhere else. She had now decided she really didn't like Essie and she certainly didn't want to be in her squad.

Even the takeaway pizza and massive bottle of cola that Essie ordered wasn't enough to change Maia's mind and she was very glad when her mum arrived to collect her.

"I'll see you tomorrow in school," Essie said. "Remember your hairslide."

Maia had no intention of wearing it so she didn't say anything.

"Did you have a nice time?" Mrs Greene asked as they walked back to the car.

"Not really. I don't much like Essie," Maia muttered.

Mrs Greene looked surprised. "That's not like you, Maia. Don't judge her too quickly. Moving here will be a big change for her. You may not be seeing the real her at the moment."

Maia wasn't convinced. She was very relieved when they got home and she could talk to Bracken.

"How was it?" he asked.

She stroked him. "Awful. I'd far rather have been meeting up with you and the other animals and Ionie and Sita. Now we've wasted a day when we could have been trying to work out what's going on."

Bracken climbed on to her knee and licked her cheek. "Don't worry. We'll go to the clearing tomorrow and see if we can find any clues then."

Her arms closed around his warm body and her bad mood faded. Bracken was right. They'd only lost one day. "I love you," she told him. "You always make me feel better."

His eyes shone and he snuggled closer. "I love you, too, Maia," he said.

Chapter Six

Maia was surprised when she got up and found her mum getting ready to go out for a run. "It's only seven o'clock!" Maia said.

Her mum nodded. "I know but I had this weird dream last night. I was taking part in the fun run and I actually finished first. Well, I woke up just wanting to go out running. I'm already faster than Ellie and Jo, even though they have done much more running than me. If I train a bit more, I think I could do quite well in this race."

Maia blinked. "But you hate running."

"I do, but it's good to push yourself," her mum said. "And every run I do means another guilt-free slice of cake at The Copper Kettle!"

"Can we go there soon?" said Maia.

Her mum smiled. "Sure. Now get some breakfast. Dad will take you to school today." She did up her trainers and set off.

Maia got ready for school. She brushed her hair but left it loose on her shoulders rather than putting it in a ponytail and she put the red hairslide in her bag.

When Lottie arrived at school, her hair was pulled into a tight, high ponytail with the red hairslide that Essie clipped into it. It looked a bit odd because her hair was only shoulder-length and so her ponytail was very short.

"Why have you got your hair like that?" Ionie said, frowning at her.

Lottie blushed. "I … um, just fancied a change." She looked at Maia. "You haven't got a ponytail."

Understanding dawned on Ionie's face as Maia shook her head. "Oh, I get it! Essie's told you to wear your hair in a particular way so that you become clones of her. That's it, isn't it?" She looked across the playground to where Tara and Sadie were greeting Essie. They all had matching high ponytails with red hairslides. "It is!" she said incredulously.

Maia sighed and nodded.

"Lottie! Maia!" Essie called, waving to them. "Over here!"

Lottie went over but Maia didn't.

"Why aren't you joining in?" Ionie said to her.

"I don't like Essie," Maia said.

"Why?" said Sita in surprise.

Maia just shrugged. She didn't want to
tell Sita what Essie had said about her. "I just
don't."

Essie came over. "Why are you hanging
around here?" she said, ignoring Sita and Ionie.
"And where's your hairslide?"

Maia rummaged in her bag and pulled it out.
"Here, you can have it back," she said. "I don't
want to wear it."

Essie's eyes hardened. "Then you can't be
in my squad."

Maia met Essie's gaze. She wasn't going to be bullied. "Fine."

Essie snatched the hair slide. "Your loss." She flicked her ponytail and flounced back to the others.

"Why *does* Lottie like her?" said Ionie in astonishment.

Maia shook her head. "I have no idea."

Lottie continued to hang around with Essie all day. Maia found it hard to understand. Yes, Essie was grown up and funny in some ways but she was also quite mean.

At the end of the day, Lottie came out with Essie and the others. Essie was imitating Mr Neal and they were all giggling.

"Lottie!" Maia called. "We're going!"

Lottie said goodbye to Essie and ran over. "Essie's so much fun," she said.

"Really?" Ionie said disbelievingly.

"You didn't seriously enjoy last night at her house, did you?" Maia said. "All that showing off and talking about make-up and boys?"

"Yes, I did enjoy it," said Lottie in surprise. "Well, most of it. Didn't you?"

"No," Maia said.

"Lottie!" They looked round. It was Lottie's mum. "Change of plan. You can't go to Ionie's tonight, I'm afraid," she said, coming over. "I'm sorry, Ionie."

"But why? You said I could go until my swimming lesson, Mum," said Lottie.

"I know, but when I woke up this morning I realized that you could be using this hour and a half more usefully," said her mum. "I think it would be a really good idea for you to learn German and I've found a tutor who can fit you in on Wednesdays."

Lottie's face fell. "Mum! I already do French plus extra maths, piano, tennis, gymnastics and trampolining."

"Yes, and now you'll be doing German and flute, too," said her mum.

"But I won't have time to see my friends!" Lottie protested.

"You'll still have a few hours free at the weekend," said her mum. "Now, come along. No arguing."

Shooting a despairing look at the others, Lottie went with her mum.

"Poor Lottie," Maia said, the irritation she'd been feeling with her friend fading instantly.

"I'd hate to have all those extra classes," said Ionie.

"I'll call in this evening and tell her what we've been doing so she doesn't feel left out," said Sita.

They headed back to Ionie's house, dumped their school bags and went to the clearing.

"Look at it!" Sita whispered, staring around horrified.

The clearing looked far worse than it had done a few days before. A dark mould was creeping up the tree trunks and even the evergreen trees had lost their needles. The leaves on the dark green ivy had turned brown and the air smelled of damp and decay.

"It's awful," Maia said. "What can have made it get so bad?"

"Dark magic," said Ionie grimly. "Let's call the animals."

They called their animals' names. When Sorrel appeared she hissed, her tail puffing up. Willow's nostrils flared.

"What is it?" Sita said in alarm.

"Shades!" said Willow, her eyes wide. "Shades have been here! I can smell them!"

CHAPTER SEVEN

"The air absolutely stinks of Shades," said
Sorrel, prowling around the decaying clearing.

Bracken looked uneasy. "I can't smell Shades
like you," he said, "but I can tell the clearing
feels wrong. The air feels heavy and dull."

"The life force is being sucked out of it,"
said Sorrel. She looked around. "Where are
Lottie and Juniper?"

"Lottie had to go with her mum," said Maia.

"I don't like it here any more," said
Willow, pushing against Sita's leg. "Can we go

somewhere else to talk?"

Bracken nodded.

"Let's go to the beach," Maia said.

They set off through the trees. The animals kept to the shadows and then vanished when they reached the clifftop, only reappearing when the girls found a sheltered spot to sit down.

The beach was made of pebbles with big boulders at the bottom of the cliffs. They found a place where the boulders made a complete circle with dry pebbles in the centre of them. There was no one anywhere nearby, just a few dog walkers and beachcombers in the distance. Overhead, seagulls wheeled across the sky.

"What are we going to do about the clearing?" said Sita.

"I'll use my magic," said Maia. She took her mirror out of her pocket. "Show me who has been conjuring Shades."

The mirror swirled but no picture formed.

"I'm not seeing anything," Maia said.

"Try asking something else," urged Sorrel.

Maia thought for a moment. "Show me where the Shades are," she tried.

But once again the mirror showed nothing.

She bit her lip. "Show me what's coming," she said.

This time, an image did appear. It was followed by another and another: the same hooded figure in the clearing; a row of glass bottles filled with dark liquid... Maia blinked... A girl with her face buried in her hands, sobbing in a bedroom; a woman with

a hammer; Maia's dad shouting angrily …
and then a Shade's evil face suddenly filled
the mirror, grotesque and large, its red eyes
gleaming. "We are here!" it hissed. "Beware!
We three shall not be beaten!" Maia gasped
and dropped the mirror on to her knees.

"What is it?" Bracken said.

Heart racing, Maia described what she had
seen.

"It said there were *three* Shades?" said Sita
anxiously.

Maia nodded. Sorrel gave a hiss and paced
around the circle of rocks they were sheltering
amongst. "This is not good."

Sita looked anxiously at Willow. "Will the
things Maia saw definitely come true?"

"Not definitely," Willow said. "The magic
shows possible future events but all of those
things can be changed."

"If we can figure out what's going on,"
said Maia.

"You said you saw the figure in the woods again," said Ionie, her face frowning in concentration. "Did it look like it might be Alice?"

Maia nodded. "It could have been." The person was about the same size and height as Alice.

"I bet it's her, or why would the magic have shown you the crystals in the shop? Try spying on her," said Ionie. "Let's see if we can find out anything more about her."

"I want to see Alice," Maia told the mirror.

She expected to see Alice in the shop and so was surprised to see a beach appear in the mirror. Alice was walking along it with a bag over her arm. She was heading for a circle of boulders by the cliffs. Maia looked up in surprise. "I think she's here!"

She jumped up and went out through the boulders on to the pebbles and saw Alice walking towards them. "It *is* her!" she

squeaked. The animals vanished, and Ionie and
Sita joined Maia.

"Hello!" Alice said, spotting them. "What a
surprise to see you girls."

"A-and you," stammered Maia. She stared
at Alice. Could she really be the person doing
dark magic and conjuring Shades?

"What are you doing here?" said
Ionie suspiciously.

"Oh, it's half-day closing at
the shop today so I thought
I'd pop down and collect
some bits and pieces
from the beach for the
beachcomber sculpture
competition," said Alice.
"I also wanted to gather
some plants and herbs
in the woods." She
nodded to the bag
on her arm.

"Plants?" Sita echoed.

"Plants can be used for magic, you know." Alice's eyes twinkled. "You can make a sleep-easy potion with lavender or a calming potion with camomile. There are all sorts of magical things you can do with plants." She tapped her nose. "Believe in magic, dearies. Remember that. Now, I'd better go. My car-park ticket is going to run out. See you in the shop soon, I hope – or maybe at the sculpture competition!" She headed off down the beach.

The girls watched her go and then disappeared back between the rocks. "We were right!" Maia hissed. "She *is* the person we're looking for!"

"She even just told us she uses plant magic!" said Sita.

"Wait a sec!" said Ionie, shaking her head. "Something about this doesn't make sense."

"What?" said Maia impatiently.

"Would she really talk about magic so

openly if she's actually doing dark magic?"
Ionie pointed out. "Wouldn't she want to keep
it secret?"

There was a pause as her words sank in.

"I guess it is a bit odd," Maia admitted.

"Mmm," said Sita. "Why would she tell us
she can do magic?"

"You know, I'm not sure about this any
more," Ionie said. "Maybe it's not her."

"But why did the magic show me the crystals
on the shelf at *Fairytales* then?" said Maia.

"And if Alice isn't the person doing dark
magic, then who is?" said Sita.

They stared at each other, puzzled. None of
them had an answer to that.

When Maia got home, her dad was sitting at
his laptop at the kitchen table.

"What's for supper?" Maia asked.

"I don't know," he said vaguely. "Mum's out

running and I've been too busy to think about it."

"What are you doing?" Maia asked curiously.

"Putting together some quiz-team practice questions," her dad said enthusiastically. "I think we could do well in this quiz. We need to get practising though, to make sure we have the best chance of beating the other teams."

"Practising?" Maia echoed.

"Yes, tomorrow night after school."

"But I'm meeting the others then," Maia protested.

Her dad shook his head. "Not tomorrow. We're going to practise. We could win this, Maia."

Clio came in with a piece of mangled toast. "I just found Alfie trying to put this in the DVD player, Dad."

Maia expected their dad to rush into the lounge but he just waved a hand. "Can you deal with it? I'm busy with these quiz questions."

Clio groaned. "Dad, it's just a little quiz in
the village hall. It's not *University Challenge*."

"Mmm." Her dad stared at the screen.

Clio shook her head at Maia. "Will you help
me? Alfie's very sticky – and so's the DVD
player."

"Sure." Wondering why her dad was quite
so obsessed with the quiz, Maia helped Clio
clean up Alfie and the DVD player then pulled
out her phone and texted Lottie.

Did u see Sita? Did she call in?

A text pinged back from Lottie.

Mum wdn't let her in. She's making me do a practice maths exam! Sita's going to Facetime me later. Can't stop now. Gotta finish this maths. Argh!

Maia shook her head. OK, her dad might be being a bit weird but Lottie's mum was a lot worse. Frustration welled up inside her. There were Shades in Westcombe. They didn't have time to do things like maths papers and quiz practice. They needed to be doing magic! She remembered the Shade's gloating face and lifted her chin.

We'll stop you, she vowed. *Just you wait and see.*

CHAPTER EIGHT

Maia arrived at school the next morning at the same time as Lottie. She could tell straight away that her friend was not in a good mood by the way she was stomping up the pathl.

"What's up?" Maia asked, falling into step beside her.

"My mum!" Lottie threw her hands in the air. "I've tried telling her I don't want to do all the extra things she has planned but she just keeps going on about how helpful it will be for my 'future career prospects' and says I'm doing the extra things whether I like it or not!"

"That's awful," said Maia sympathetically.

"She's so controlling!" Lottie burst out. "I want to come and meet you tonight but she says I have to fit in more piano practice and tomorrow she's taking me to meet my new flute teacher. Sita Facetimed me and told me what happened yesterday and I know I need to be with all of you." Tears sprang into her eyes and she blinked them away.

Maia hugged her. There wasn't much she could say. "We'll meet up Saturday lunchtime like normal, as soon as you've finished gymnastics." She lowered her voice. "And try to track down the you-know-whos then."

"Lottie!" Essie breezed up with Sadie. She ignored Maia. "Do you want to come round to my house tomorrow night?"

"I can't," sighed Lottie. "I've got a flute lesson."

"How about Saturday then?" Essie said.

"Come round in the morning and we can hang out at mine all day."

"Count me in," said Sadie with feeling. "My mum just told me she wants me to spend Saturday morning on the beach helping her find things to add to her beach sculpture for that competition thing. No. Thank. You."

"I can't come round first thing. I've got gymnastics," said Lottie.

"Come afterwards then," Essie said.

"Lottie always meets me, Sita and Ionie after gymnastics on a Saturday," Maia put in.

It was as if she hadn't spoken. Essie's eyes didn't flicker from Lottie's face. "You do want to be my friend, don't you, Lottie?" she said. Her voice sounded sweet but there was a knife-sharp edge to it.

"Yes, of course!" Lottie said.

"Then you'll come to mine," said Essie with a confident smile. "Now," she hooked her arm through Lottie's, "let's go and talk about what

we'll do on Saturday."
She dragged Lottie
away.

Lottie gave Maia an
apologetic look over
her shoulder. Maia
felt a rush of anger
and marched into the
playground.

"Are you OK?" Sita
said, seeing her face.

Maia shook her head.
"No! I was talking to Lottie when Essie came
along and then Lottie went off with her. I
think she might even be going to Essie's on
Saturday after gymnastics rather than meeting
up with us. I can't believe it!"

Ionie's mouth fell open. "But we *have* to
meet then! There's so much we need to do."

"I know!" Maia exclaimed.

"Lottie won't let us down," said Sita

quickly. "She'll meet us. I'm sure she will."

"Hmm." Maia wasn't convinced.

Clio was making a sandwich when Maia got home that afternoon. "How was school today?"

"OK, I guess." Maia shrugged.

Clio frowned. "What's up?"

Maia poured herself a glass of juice from the fridge. Clio could be annoying but she was usually pretty good when it came to advice about friends. "It's Lottie," she admitted. "She's hanging around with this new girl, Essie, and the other popular girls in Year Six. I don't get it. All they're into is boys and make-up and stuff like that."

Clio shrugged. "Maybe Lottie's into that too now she's getting older. People change in Year Six and start to like different things."

"Not me and my friends," said Maia.

"It sounds like Lottie is into that. It's really

quite normal. I wouldn't stress about it." Clio stretched. "So what time do you think Dad wants to do this practice?"

"I don't know but I hope he doesn't make us practise for too long." Maia sighed.

She went upstairs. Lying on her bed with Bracken, she cuddled him and told him about her day.

"Essie sounds horrible," he said, snuffling her neck. "Lottie's being silly. You're a million times nicer."

Maia smiled. Bracken always understood. "I'm glad I've got you, Bracken."

He snuggled closer and cocked his head to one side. "Could Lottie be behaving strangely and wanting to be this girl's friend because of a Shade?"

Maia had been wondering that, too. "I don't know. I don't really think so. She's not being mean or horrible or anything like that, she just likes hanging around with Essie, and Clio told me it's normal for people to change in Year Six."

"It might be worth getting Sorrel or Willow to check Lottie's house for Shades though," said Bracken. "Just in case."

Maia nodded. "Good plan. Well, that's if Lottie's mum ever lets us in!"

"Maia!" her dad called. "Time to do some quiz practice!"

Maia kissed Bracken on the nose. "I'd better go. See you later," she said and then she went reluctantly downstairs.

The quiz practice was not fun. Maia's dad kept going over and over the general knowledge questions until Maia was so bored she thought she might explode.

Even worse, he then insisted on yet another practice on Friday night straight after school, which meant Maia wasn't able to meet up with Ionie and Sita. Maia had never known him act like this before. She thought about the image she'd seen of her dad when she'd been using magic. He'd been shouting at someone. Could it be something to do with this quiz?

On Saturday, Maia got up and found her dad in the kitchen surrounded by cups of half-drunk coffee. He was reading over fresh question sheets he'd printed off the internet.

Maia got herself a bowl of cereal. She was just about to pour the milk when there was a knock at the front door.

Her dad answered it.

Hearing him talking to someone, Maia went

through to the hall. It was
their elderly neighbour,
Mr Jones. He looked
very upset. "You didn't
hear anything then,
David?" he was saying
to Maia's dad. "It must
have happened between
midnight and six o'clock
this morning. I can't
believe it. After all the work
I put in."

"What's happened?" Maia asked
curiously.

Her dad looked shocked. "You know the
sculpture Mr Jones has been making for the
competition?"

Maia nodded. Mr Jones usually won and this
year she knew he had been making a beautiful
swan out of driftwood and sea-glass. She'd seen
it from her bedroom window.

"Someone came into his garden and destroyed it during the night!" her dad said.

"That's awful!" gasped Maia.

"They just smashed it up," said Mr Jones, shaking his head. "The judging is this afternoon so I can't make another. I mean, who would do something like that? I spent hours making it."

"Did you hear anything outside, Maia?" her dad asked.

"No."

"I'll go and see if Pete and Doreen on the other side noticed anything," said Mr Jones.

Maia hurried upstairs, her breakfast forgotten. Maybe she could use magic to find out who had damaged the sculpture! Shutting her bedroom door, she sat down at her desk and looked into the mirror. She breathed deeply and magic swirled into her, warm and tingly.

"Show me what happened to Mr Jones's sculpture," she said.

An image appeared of the next-door garden in the pale grey light of dawn. The beautiful swan sculpture was on the garden table. Someone opened the gate and came in. Who was it? To Maia's surprise she saw a short, dark-haired woman. Maia frowned. She was sure it was a mum she recognized from the playground, although she wasn't quite sure whose mum she was. In shock, she watched as the woman pulled out a hammer from under her coat.

Maia's eyes widened. No! She'd seen this before! It was the woman she'd seen when she'd asked the magic to show her the future!

"I *will* win!" the woman muttered and then she started hitting the delicate sculpture with the hammer. It fell to bits.

She glanced round swiftly and then tucked the hammer back under her coat and hurried out of the gate.

Maia wondered what she should do. She couldn't tell Mr Jones what she knew – she didn't have any proof he would believe. For a second, she wondered if the woman could be the person doing dark magic in the clearing but she was too short and her hair was brown. It was far more likely that she was being affected by one of the Shades they knew were in Westcombe. Why else would she just attack the sculpture? Maia had never heard about her being mean or horrible before.

Maia took a deep breath. She had to tell the others and they could try and find out more. It looked like it was going to be a very exciting day!

CHAPTER NINE

Maia went downstairs. Her mum was talking to her dad in the hall. "Ellie's out of the race! She's hurt her ankle," she was saying.

"Mmm," Mr Greene said, hardly listening as he leaned against the wall, reading quiz papers.

"Mum!" Maia said, shocked. "You sound almost pleased that Ellie's hurt herself."

"Well, it means one less person to beat!" her mum said. A strange greedy look crossed her face. "Imagine if more people got injured. That would be good."

"What?" Maia stared. Her mum would never usually say something so mean.

"Just saying," her mum said with a sly smile. "I'd be more likely to win."

Maia edged away. This wasn't right. Why was her mum acting like this?

Shade! her mind screamed at her. It seemed the only possible explanation for her mum's nasty behaviour.

Maia's throat felt dry. Could there be a Shade in *her* house?

"I'm going out," she said suddenly.

Her dad looked up. "You can't. You need to revise for this quiz!"

"But I'm going to Ionie's," Maia said.

"No!" her dad's voice rose angrily. "You have to stay! You can't go out!"

Maia's heart flipped. What was going on? Her dad never shouted! It was just as she'd seen in the mirror!

"Stay here!" he yelled.

Maia didn't listen. She dashed to the front door and was through it and out before he could stop her. "See you later!" she gasped and then she set off, running down the road.

By the time she reached Ionie's she was pink in the face and gasping for breath.

"Are you OK?" Ionie said, coming to the door with Sita.

"No…" panted Maia. "Mum… Dad… Shades."

Ionie and Sita gave each other alarmed looks. "Let's go upstairs," Ionie said quickly.

They hurried to Ionie's room. "Lottie texted this morning – she'll be here soon," said Ionie.

"What's happened, Maia?" Sita said.

"Call the animals first," said Maia.

Bracken sensed there was something wrong as soon as he appeared. "What's the matter?" he said, bounding anxiously over to Maia. "You don't look happy."

Maia told them what had happened that morning. "I thought Mum and Dad were just being a bit weird but now I'm sure they're being affected by Shades. And that woman I saw who smashed up Mr Jones's sculpture. Why would she do something like that? Maybe she did it because of a Shade as well."

"So we're dealing with a type of Shade that only affects adults by the looks of it," said Sorrel. "A Shade that makes people want to win and beat others."

"At all costs," said Maia with a shudder, thinking of the woman with the hammer and the creepy look in her mum's eyes as she had talked about people getting injured. "We have to find where the Shades are." She ran a hand through her hair. Three Shades – one in her house, maybe one in the woman's and then one somewhere else.

"Should we go back to yours?" said Bracken.

Maia hesitated. "I don't know. Dad was really mad. He might try to lock me in."

"Well, why don't we go to the sculpture competition instead?" said Ionie. "It's being judged this afternoon in the beach car park. I bet the woman who destroyed Mr Jones's sculpture will be there. We might find something out from her. Come on. They'll be setting up now." She jumped to her feet.

"Shouldn't we wait for Lottie?" said Sita. Her phone pinged. "Oh, it's from her." Sita held out her phone and they all read Lottie's message.

"That's it?" Ionie exclaimed. "That's all we get?"

"I bet she's gone to Essie's!" said Maia. Anger flashed through her. There wasn't a kiss or an emoji with the text. There certainly wasn't an explanation. How could Lottie let them down like this? They needed her – really needed her.

"She says she can't come round *now*," said Sita hopefully. "That might mean she'll come round in a bit. Let's wait a while longer."

Maia and Ionie reluctantly agreed but when Lottie hadn't appeared after another twenty minutes, Maia jumped to her feet.

"This is stupid," she said. "We can't just sit around all day. She's obviously not coming."

Ionie nodded. "I think we should go."

"OK." Sita sighed.

They headed out of the house and down the lane. There was music coming from the open windows of Essie's house as they walked past. "I wish Essie had never moved in," Maia muttered, thinking of Lottie inside. How could she abandon them to be with Essie and the others?

Just as they reached the clifftop they heard a voice calling their names. They looked round and saw Lottie jogging down the lane towards them. "Sorry I couldn't meet you earlier," she panted as she reached them. "Did you get my message?"

"Yes," Maia said shortly.

Ionie folded her arms. "So you saw us passing Essie's house and thought you might finally come and join us then?"

Lottie frowned. "What?"

Maia lost her temper. "I can't believe you dumped us to go and hang around with her! We've had enough, Lottie. You can't be friends with her and us – you're going to have to choose!"

"I didn't dump you!" Lottie protested. "I've

come straight from the new German lessons my mum is making me do. I tried to send a message telling you I'd be another thirty minutes but before I could finish it Mum took my phone off me." She glared at them. "Did you really think I'd go round to Essie's rather than come and do magic when there's important stuff happening, stuff we need to deal with?" Her voice rose. "And even if you did think that, who are you to tell me who I can and can't be friends with?"

"Lottie, we're sorry." Sita stepped towards her while Ionie and Maia stared open-mouthed.

"No. Don't use your magic on me, Sita!" Lottie snapped. "I've changed my mind. I don't want to be with you this afternoon, after all! I'm going home!" Turning, she ran back up the lane.

"Wait!" Maia shouted, racing after her but Lottie used her magic and vanished in the blink of an eye. Maia stared at the empty space where Lottie had been standing and then turned. Sita was biting her lip and trying not to cry.

"Oh dear. I think we owe her an apology," Ionie said slowly.

Maia nodded. Her anger had disappeared as quickly as it had blown up and now she just felt awful.

"Should we go after her?" Sita said.

"We'll never catch her if she's using her magic," said Maia.

"I could shadow-travel us to her house," said Ionie.

"I don't know. Maybe we should give her a bit of space," said Maia doubtfully, remembering how angry Lottie had been. When Lottie got cross she tended to stay cross for quite a long time. She pulled out her phone and texted her instead.

> We're really sorry. Can we come round?
> Mxxxxxxx

"Let's wait to get a reply," she said.

Sita nodded. "I think that's best."

"Let's go to the competition for now then," said Ionie. "Hopefully she'll text us back soon."

They reached the clifftop. From there a walkway led down to the beach. On one side of it was a small open-air car park. Usually in February there were only a few cars but today it was packed with vehicles. There was a big canvas sign stretched across the entrance saying *Westcombe Beachcomber Sculpture Competition* in large letters, and tables were set up around the car park where competitors were laying out the sculptures they had made from things they had found on the beach. Another sign announced that the judging would begin at 2 p.m.

Maia looked round at all the people – some were drinking coffee, others chatting, others wandering from table to table admiring the sculptures. She nudged Ionie and Maia. "There's Alice," she whispered, seeing the shop owner fussing around her entry – a gorgeous driftwood dragon with green sea glass for eyes and shells for scales.

"Should we go over?" Ionie whispered. "We have to find out if she knows about the Shades or not."

"How do we do that?" said Maia.

"I know!" said Sita, suddenly looking determined. "It's time to sort this out once and for all. Follow me."

Maia and Ionie exchanged surprised looks. It wasn't like Sita to lead the way but they followed her over to Alice's table.

Alice beamed at them. "Hello, dearies. Have you been having a look around? Aren't the other entries amazing?"

"Yours is really good, too," said Maia politely. "I really like the—"

"Alice, I need to talk to you," Sita interrupted, her hazel eyes serious. She dropped her voice. "Now, you must listen to me and answer with the truth."

Maia gaped. She knew Sita was using her ability to command people to do anything she wanted. She also knew that Sita hated using that power.

Alice blinked. "I shall," she said obediently.

Sita stepped closer. "Have you been using dark magic?" she asked.

Maia glanced around. Luckily everyone nearby was busy and no one was listening.

Alice looked confused. "Dark magic? No. Just good magic. Sleep-easy potions, energizing oils, healing creams. I collect herbs. I make potions. People buy them and they help."

The girls exchanged looks. So Sorrel had been right when she said she felt magic in the shop. But someone else was responsible for the dark magic in the clearing.

"When I click my fingers you won't have to answer my questions any more," said Sita. "And you will forget what I have just been doing."

Alice nodded. "I shall forget," she repeated.

Sita clicked her fingers. Alice's face cleared. She looked confused for a second. "Sorry, dearie," she said, shaking her head. "Did you just ask me a question?"

"I just asked how long it took you to make the dragon," Sita said. "He's great."

"Thank you. I've been working on him for weeks," said Alice.

"Good luck," said Maia.

"Thank you, dearie," trilled Alice.

They moved away. They couldn't talk about what had just happened with so many people around but Maia was sure the others were thinking the same as her. If Alice wasn't doing dark magic, who was? Suddenly she caught sight of a short, dark-haired woman. She had a messy sculpture of a house on the table and she was glaring around at all the other competitors and muttering under her breath.

"It's her!" Maia hissed. Grabbing Sita's and Ionie's arms, she stared at the woman. "That's the woman I saw!"

"That's Mrs Varley, Sadie's mum," said Ionie.

"Don't come near!" Sadie's mum snapped as a mum and boy went over to see her sculpture. "Only the judges can come close. Go away!"

"She's acting really oddly," said Ionie.

"Look at this one, Mum." The boy who had just been told to go away pulled his mum over to Alice's table. "This is definitely the best!"

Maia caught her breath as she saw a look of utter fury cross Sadie's mum's face.

"No!" Sadie's mum hissed to herself. "Mine's the best. Mine will win." She picked up some scissors.

"Quick!" Maia gasped, fear jolting through her. What if Sadie's mum did something awful? "We have to get those scissors. Oh, why isn't Lottie here?" Lottie could have used her super-speed to grab the scissors in a second.

"I know what to do!" Ionie said and she whispered Sorrel's name. The cat suddenly appeared. She looked round in surprise at all the people. Ionie whispered something to her and then they hurried towards Mrs Varley. Sorrel leaped on to the table containing Mrs Varley's structure.

"No!" Mrs Varley gasped. "Get away, cat!"
She dropped the scissors and started flapping
her hands. Ionie grabbed the scissors and
pocketed them as Sorrel darted from one side
of the sculpture to the other.

"I'll get it," said Ionie, scooping Sorrel up.
"Sorry!" She hurried back to the others, the
scissors bulging in her pocket.

"It?" Sorrel hissed under her breath. "You
called me *it*?"

"Shh," Ionie whispered. People were already
looking at them. "Sorry, she's my cat. I'd better

take her home," she called to everyone.

Ionie hastily left the car park with Maia and Sita.

"Well done for getting the scissors," said Sita as they hurried back up the lane.

"I thought Mrs Varley was going to destroy someone else's sculpture with them!" said Ionie. "The grown-ups are getting totally out of control! We have to find out where these Shades are, right now. If we can send them back to the shadows then the hold they have will break and everyone they're affecting will return to normal."

"Before anyone gets seriously hurt!" said Maia, her heart racing.

"I think we should go to Lottie," said Sita. "We need her."

Ionie nodded. "Can you see where she is with your magic, Maia?"

Maia got out her mirror and looked into it. "Lottie," she said.

An image formed. It showed Lottie in her bedroom, rattling the door handle. "Mum! Let me out!" she was shouting.

"No," Lottie's mother's voice came through the door. "You can stay in there and work on your maths paper. Ninety-two per cent is not good enough. You will do it again and get a hundred per cent, and you can forget all about going out this evening!"

"Lottie's been locked in her room," Maia said. She saw Lottie fighting back tears as she slumped down on her bed.

Pulling out her phone, Lottie dialled a number. "Hi, Essie, it's me," she said a moment later. "I can't come round this evening." There was a silence. "I'm sorry, I just can't. It's my mum. She's making me do a load of work... No, I can't change her mind. She's being awful, Essie." Lottie's voice broke with a sob. "I'm feeling scared of her and..." She broke off and then her shoulders slumped.

"OK. I get it, you've got to go. I'll see you Monday at school." She clicked the phone off, threw it down and buried her head in her hands and started to cry.

"We've got to go to her!" said Maia. It was horrible seeing Lottie so unhappy. "Maybe *her* mum is being affected by Shades, too. She's normally a little bit nuts but now she's being full-on crazy!"

Ionie ran to a patch of shadows under a tree at the side of the lane with Sorrel bounding beside her. "Come on," she said, holding out her hands.

Sita and Maia ran and grabbed hold of a hand each and the next moment they felt themselves spinning away.

Chapter Ten

As their feet hit carpet, they heard a sharp intake of breath. Maia saw Lottie staring at them from her bed. "What are you doing here?" she demanded.

Maia squeezed out from the gap beside the wardrobe and went over to her. "Lottie, I'm really sorry... I shouldn't have accused you of going to Essie's instead of meeting us."

"We are all sorry," said Sita, joining her.

"We want to apologize," said Ionie.

"You should have known I wouldn't do

that!" said Lottie reproachfully.

"I know," said Maia.

"And we are all really, really sorry," said Ionie. "But right now there's other stuff going on we absolutely have to deal with and we need you!" She looked at the door. "Has your mum locked you in?"

Lottie wiped away her tears. "She's gone crazy. She wants me to redo a maths paper and I'm not allowed out until I get every question right. I don't know what's up with her!"

"It's a Shade," said Ionie. "The Shades that are in Westcombe are making adults really competitive."

"It's why my mum wants to beat everyone in the fun run and why my dad has gone loopy over a family quiz," said Maia. "Oh, and also why Sadie's mum destroyed Mr Jones's sculpture – she wants to win the beachcomber competition so badly. Just now we had to stop her attacking someone else's sculpture with scissors!"

Lottie stared at her wide-eyed. "So it's not just my mum being a crazy control-freak?"

"Nope," said Maia. "This is all because of dark magic and we need to sort it out. Should we call the animals?"

"Yes," Lottie said. "Mum won't come back for a while. She thinks I'm doing the maths paper." A look of relief crossed her face. "Thanks for coming. I was so cross with you all. I didn't think I wanted to see any of you but really I did. I tried telling Essie how horrible Mum was being but she just said she was busy and hung up."

Maia remembered the phone conversation she'd overheard. "So you were planning on seeing her *after* you met up with us?" she said.

"Yes, you'll always come first – you and magic. But I do have fun hanging round with Essie and the others, and I don't want to have to choose between you," Lottie said, looking upset.

Maia took a deep breath. "I shouldn't have said you had to." She realized she'd been guilty of being just as controlling as Lottie's mum and felt a rush of guilt. "You can be friends with Essie as well as us. It's fine."

Lottie smiled and hugged her. "Thank you, but you three will always be my best friends. And Juniper, too, of course! Now, let's call the animals and see if we can work out what's going on!"

Soon, they were all sitting around on Lottie's bedroom floor trying to think what the three Shades might be trapped in. The animals cuddled up to the girls.

"We need to think of something that's in Maia's house, Lottie's house and Sadie's house," Ionie said. "What have you recently got?"

"We all bought stuff at *Fairytales*." Maia realized she had the friendship bracelet on and held her arm out. "Here, does it smell of Shades?"

"And what about the dragon egg I got?" said Lottie, jumping up and getting it from her desk.

Sorrel and Willow sniffed both but then shook their heads.

"So what else do you two have that's new?" said Ionie.

"The red hairslides Essie gave us!" Lottie said, spotting hers on her desk. "What about those?"

Maia shook her head. "No, I gave mine back to Essie." She thought back over the images she'd seen with magic. The hooded figure … the clearing … the bottles of potion … the crystals on the shelf with the colourful dreamcatchers behind…

"Dreamcatchers!" she gasped. "Essie gave us dreamcatchers!" She stared at the others, her hands flying to her mouth. "Oh no! I've been so stupid! I thought the magic was showing me the crystals on the shelf at *Fairytales* but it wasn't the crystals that were important, it was the turquoise and pink dreamcatchers hanging up behind them! I've got one, so has Lottie and so has Sadie!"

"But Sorrel would have smelled Shades in them in *Fairytales*," argued Ionie.

"There were definitely no Shades there then," said Sorrel.

"Esther could have bought them before we went in," said Maia. "Don't you remember?

When we got there, Alice was re-stocking them! She said they had been selling like hot cakes. I bet Esther had just been in and bought a load of them and the three turquoise and pink ones had Shades in."

"But why? Who put them there?" said Juniper, jumping on to Lottie's bed in agitation.

"I don't know but what's important now is getting our hands on those three dreamcatchers, and sending the Shades back to the shadows before one of the adults does something really bad!" said Maia.

"Where's yours, Lottie?" said Sita.

"On the landing outside my bedroom."

They looked at the locked door.

"How are we going to get it?" Maia said.

Lottie smiled. "Mum might have locked me in but there are other ways out of this room than through the door!" She ran to the window, opened it and a second later was climbing out. "Back in a minute!"

In fact she returned in less than a minute, the blue dreamcatcher in her hand as she climbed back in through the window. She jumped down to the floor. "Here it is," she said, throwing it on to her rug.

Sorrel and Willow walked cautiously towards it but then both jumped back, Sorrel with a hiss, Willow with her nostrils flaring.

"Shade!" Sorrel spat.

"Are you sure?" Ionie said.

"Without a doubt," said Sorrel.

"Yes. There's definitely a Shade in it," said Willow nervously.

"What do we do?" said Lottie.

"Sita, you command the Shade out from the dreamcatcher – it will have to do whatever you say – and then I will order it to go back to the Shadows," said Ionie. She was a Spirit Speaker, a special kind of Star Friend who could banish Shades back to the Shadow World.

"Remember, you need to be looking it in the eyes to send it back to the shadows," Sorrel said.

"I know," Ionie said impatiently. "But Sita can command it to look at me."

"Are you ready, Sita?" Maia said.

Sita took a deep breath. "I command you to come out, Shade," she said, staring at the dreamcatcher. "Show yourself."

For a moment nothing happened and then a shadow seemed to move over the surface of the dreamcatcher. It swirled faster and faster, like a mini tornado, and then burst upwards towards the girls and animals. As it did so, the smoke formed into a tall, thin shape with long

arms, spiny fingers, sharp teeth and red eyes.
Maia felt a shiver run down her spine and saw
Sita's face turn pale.

"Free at last!" the Shade hissed.

"I want you to freez—" Sita started to speak
but before she could finish commanding it the
Shade had leaped towards her. It clamped its
hand over her mouth, stifling her words.

"Let her go!" Maia gasped as Sita struggled
frantically in its grip.

"Oh no." Its mouth widened into a gloating smile. "Did you think I couldn't hear you talking while I was in the dreamcatcher? I could hear every word. I know to avoid that one's gaze." It nodded at Ionie while not looking directly into her eyes. "And I know that this one is dangerous. Well, she shall not command me. In the catcher I could only affect a few people. Now I am free, I will go where I wish."

"To do what?" demanded Lottie.

The Shade smiled evilly. "To cause unhappiness and bring discord. I will talk to people in their sleep, bring them dreams that feed their ambitions, make them dream a future where they could win and lead them to a point where they will hurt anyone who stands in their way," it sneered. "It is easily done. Whisper words in their ears and soon their personality starts to change..."

"But only adults can hear you?" said Maia.

"Yes, only adults," the Shade agreed.

"Why would you do it?" said Lottie.

"Because every time I do something evil, I grow stronger," hissed the Shade.

Sita struggled under the Shade's hand.

"Let Sita go!" Maia said through gritted teeth.

"No," said the Shade. Maia and Ionie both stepped towards it. "Stop there. If you come near me I shall hurt her." It flexed its vicious fingernails and drew a faint line across Sita's neck. Pinpricks of blood welled up where his razor-sharp nails touched her skin.

Sita struggled desperately. "Stay still!" it snapped. "Or I shall do worse!" It looked at the others. "You are going to let me go free. If anyone tries to stop me, this girl will suffer." It edged away, its angular bones clicking as it dragged Sita with it. Maia knew they had to stop it! It couldn't be allowed to affect lots of people, while getting stronger and stronger all the time. Her mind flicked through all the things they could do. The only way to stop it was to free

Sita so she could command it but how could they do that? A plan suddenly came to her.

Using her magic, she saw the Shade's outline move a second before it made the move for real. Its hand was reaching for the window. "You're not going anywhere!" she cried, leaping forwards and barrelling into the Shade with her shoulder, knocking it away from the open window. "And if you want to hurt someone, you can hurt me not Sita!"

The Shade lost its grip on Sita. She took the opportunity to tear herself free. With a snarl, the Shade grabbed Maia and slashed its hands at her. She gasped and ducked, hiding her face. She'd been ready for the pain – expecting it – but it still hurt. Its talons raked down her arm and she cried out. Bracken snarled in fury and grabbed its leg while Juniper leaped at its head, Willow butted its arm and Sorrel dug her claws into its foot but the Shade took no notice. It lifted its hand. It was going to slash her face!

"Stop hurting Maia!" Sita shouted, scrabbling to her feet. "Stop it now!" The Shade's hand froze in mid-air. It had to do as Sita commanded.

Pushing Maia away in disgust, it leaped for the window.

But Lottie reached the window first with her super-speed and slammed it shut. "You're not going anywhere!" she cried.

Sita stared at Maia. Blood was trickling from her arm. "What's it done to you, Maia?"

"Don't worry about me!" Maia said, holding the wound. "Just send it back to the Shadows!"

"I order you to face Ionie!" Sita commanded.

The Shade tried to fight against the command but Sita's power was too strong. Its body shook with anger as it reluctantly turned to Ionie. She marched up to it. "You hurt Maia!" she said furiously.

The Shade glared at her. "I shall hurt you all!" it hissed.

"Oh no, you won't," said Ionie. "Your time here is done, Mr Spiny Fingers. Go back to the shadows. I command it!"

The Shade's body started to dissolve in grey smoke. It faded faster and faster until the last few wisps of smoke chased each other in a circle and disappeared with a pop like water going down a plughole.

"It's gone," said Lottie in relief.

"Oh my goodness, Maia." Sita threw

herself down beside her friend. "That was so brave. You saved me." Blood was seeping out from under Maia's fingers. "But look what it's done to you."

"It's OK, you can use your magic to heal me," Maia said, gritting her teeth. "I knew we couldn't defeat it unless you were free."

"So you made it attack you instead," said Ionie, her eyes wide. "That was really brave."

"Help Maia, please, Sita," Bracken begged.

Sita crouched down and gently looked at the wound the Shade had made with its nails. She put her hand just above the wound and concentrated hard. Maia felt a pleasant tingling sensation sweep over her skin. She watched as the blood dried up and the marks got smaller and smaller, shrinking to tiny scratches and then disappearing altogether, just leaving her skin slightly pink.

The pain vanished. "You made it better!" she said, hugging Sita. "Thank you."

Bracken jumped around excitedly and licked Willow on the nose. Juniper raced across the curtain pole and even Sorrel gave a satisfied purr.

"Now we need to get our hands on the other two dreamcatchers," Sita said.

They heard footsteps outside Lottie's room. "Lottie?" It was her mum.

The animals disappeared instantly. Ionie gestured to Sita and Maia to go to the shadows beside the wardrobe with her.

"Wait. I'll try to get rid of her," Lottie whispered. "Yes?" she called to her mum.

There was the sound of a key turning in the lock and the door handle moved. Lottie stepped out on to the landing, holding the door shut behind her.

"Lottie, I'm sorry." Her mum sounded strained. "I don't know what came over me this afternoon. I should never have locked you in here, and making you redo that maths paper for the sake of eight percent was a really stupid idea. I have no idea why I said it. I've been feeling so strange the last few days. It's like I've had a voice in my head making me feel it was really important you did well. I was downstairs just now and it was as if a cloud had suddenly cleared. I've been pushing you much too much. I'm sorry."

"Does this mean you're not going to make me do all those extra classes?" Lottie asked hopefully.

"No, you don't have to do them and of course you can go and see your friends this afternoon."

"Thanks, Mum!" They could hear the smile in Lottie's voice. "I'll just get my things."

She shut the door and the others stepped out from behind the wardrobe.

"Did you hear all that?" Lottie asked.

They nodded. "One dreamcatcher down, two to go!" Maia said.

First, Maia used her magic to see where
Sadie's dreamcatcher was – it was hanging
in her bedroom window – then Lottie went
downstairs and told her mum she was going
to Maia's house.

The girls all met up outside and walked to
Sadie's house. It was a detached house slightly
set back from the road. Maia had seen that
Sadie's room was on the top floor. There was a
horse chestnut tree outside it and the window
was slightly open.

"Sadie will be at Essie's so we should be safe
to get in," said Lottie. "I'll call Juniper and he
will help me. We'll climb the tree and then he
can get in through the window and pass the
dreaamcatcher out to me."

While the others kept watch, Lottie raced
to the house. They saw the branches of the
tree move as she climbed up it and then

there was a blur of red as Juniper leaped from the branches on to the windowsill and vanished inside, reappearing with the purple dreamcatcher in his mouth. He gave it to Lottie and she was back beside them in next to no time.

"Got it!" She grinned. "I can put it back later when we've got rid of the Shade!"

"Just mine to get now!" said Maia.

Not long afterwards, the girls and their animals were staring at Sadie's and Maia's dreamcatchers on the floor in Maia's room.

"How do we do this?" said Lottie.

"I'll command the Shades to come out," said Sita confidently. "Only this time I'll be ready and they won't get the better of us." She stared at the dreamcatchers. "Here goes. Shades, I command you to leave the dreamcatchers and to freeze as soon as you are out."

Grey smoke swirled from the dreamcatchers, swirling faster and faster as it formed two tall, thin shapes.

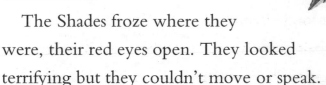

"Freeze without saying a word!" Sita commanded.

The Shades froze where they were, their red eyes open. They looked terrifying but they couldn't move or speak.

Ionie pointed at them. "Oh dear, we spoiled your little game. Now, return to the shadows!" she ordered.

The Shades' eyes flashed with fury but they had to obey and they disappeared in a puff of grey smoke.

"We've done it!" cried Lottie.

Maia felt an overwhelming rush of relief. "I can't believe it." She looked around. "They've really gone."

"We're so awesome!" said Ionie, high-fiving her. "It's all over!"

"Well, not really," Sita pointed out. "We still have to find out who trapped those Shades in the first place."

"Yes, and stop them conjuring more Shades," said Maia.

Bracken jumped into Maia's arms. "I'm up for the challenge!"

Maia buried her face in his soft fur. "And me!" she declared. "But for now, I really need some food. I didn't have any lunch and I'm starving."

"Me, too," said Lottie. "Mum didn't even give me a chance to have lunch."

"I'll get us some food," Maia said.

She went downstairs to the kitchen. Her mum was sitting at the table in her running gear having a cup of tea.

"Are you going running, Mum?" Maia said, wondering how her mum would be now the Shade had gone. People usually forgot everything that had happened when Shades returned to the shadows.

Mrs Greene sighed. "I should do really but I just don't feel like it any more. I think I've been taking this fun run far too seriously." She held out an arm and Maia went over. Her mum hugged her. "I've hardly seen you this week. Now, weren't you saying you'd like to go to The Copper Kettle the other day? How about we stop at the beachcomber competition to see who's won and then go on to the café for tea? I'll treat you, your friends and Alfie to sandwiches, hot chocolate and cake. How does that sound?"

"Awesome!" Maia said.

"Did someone mention cake?" Her dad put his head hopefully round the kitchen door.

"Yes, we're all off to The Copper Kettle," said Mrs Greene.

"Count me in!" Mr Greene said. "I am so fed up with looking at all these quiz questions!" He crumpled up the paper in his hand and tossed it aside. "It's like I've had a voice in my head telling me to keep on practising, keep on revising. It's even been there in my dreams. And what's it all for? It's going to be a good family fun night out, win or lose. No more practising, that's what I say.

Let's go out and eat cake!"

Maia grinned in delight. "I'll get the others!" she said.

They all piled into the Greenes' people-carrier. Mrs Greene took a detour to the beach car park on the way to The Copper Kettle. The judging had just taken place and Alice was beaming beside the first-place rosette next to her sculpture.

"Well done," said Maia, going over to her. She felt bad now that she'd suspected Alice of being the person doing dark magic.

"Thank you, dearie. I'm thrilled!" Alice winked and whispered, "Those little fairies at the bottom of my garden did a very good job, didn't they?"

Maia smiled. She wished Alice would stop talking to her as if she was five years old but she could see now that she meant well and it was just her way of being friendly. Maybe one day they would get her to tell them more about the plant magic she did.

Sadie's mum hadn't won anything but she didn't seem to mind. "The winners were all so good," Maia heard her saying. "I enjoyed making my sculpture anyway."

Even Mr Jones seemed happy. He'd been asked to help judge the competition and he was standing with the other three judges laughing and joking as they had a cup of tea. "Next year I'll be back with something even better!" he was saying.

"You've got to give everyone else a chance

every once in a while," joked one of the other judges.

After looking at all the beautiful sculptures, Maia and the others set off for The Copper Kettle. The cosy café was warm inside, the air filled with the smell of cake and coffee beans.

"Mmm," said Maia, breathing in deeply.

"Hello, everyone," said Mary, the owner. "One table or two?"

"I'm sure the girls would rather sit by themselves if you've got space," said Mrs Greene.

"Of course," said Mary. "No problem at all. Follow me, girls." She showed Maia, Lottie, Ionie and Sita to a large round table with comfy armchairs tucked away round the corner in an alcove, while Mr and Mrs Greene picked up some crayons and a colouring book for Alfie, grabbed a couple of newspapers and sat down at a smaller table in the window.

Soon they were all eating a delicious tea

of ham, cheese and tuna sandwiches with the crusts cut off, fruit scones, mini cupcakes covered with frosting, little chocolate brownies, and slices of apple and strawberries.

"This is the best tea ever!" said Lottie happily.

"We deserve it," declared Ionie. "It's been a very busy day."

"A busy, *magical* day," said Maia. They all grinned. "I think I know some others who deserve tea, too," she went on. She nodded to the large table covered with a tablecloth. "There's plenty of food left," she whispered. "We could call the animals. If they hide under the table no one will know they're here!"

The girls exchanged mischievous looks. They knew they shouldn't but they all wanted to!

They checked that Mary was busy talking to a customer, then they called their animals' names. The four animals appeared in a shimmer of light and looked around in surprise.

"Quick! Under the table!" Maia whispered. They all bounded under the tablecloth.

Soon, Bracken and Sorrel were eating ham and tuna sandwiches while Willow ate the apple and Juniper nibbled on a strawberry. The girls could feel their soft bodies pressing against their legs.

Maia slipped her hand under the table and stroked Bracken's fluffy head, feeling happiness rush through her. They still had a lot to find out, but right now all that mattered was that she was with her best friends and their animals, and everyone was safe.

"This really *is* the best tea ever!" she said with a smile.

Star Friends

Secret Spell

LINDA CHAPMAN

ILLUSTRATED BY LUCY FLEMING

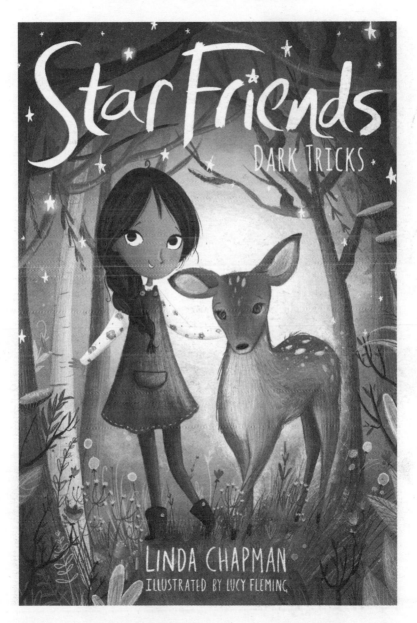

Star Friends

Dark Tricks

LINDA CHAPMAN

ILLUSTRATED BY LUCY FLEMING

About the Author

Linda Chapman is the best-selling author of over 200 books. The biggest compliment Linda can have is for a child to tell her they became a reader after reading one of her books. Linda lives in a cottage with a tower in Leicestershire with her husband, three children, three dogs and three ponies. When she's not writing, Linda likes to ride, read and visit schools and libraries to talk to people about writing.

www.lindachapmanauthor.co.uk

About the Illustrator

Lucy Fleming has been an avid doodler and bookworm since early childhood. Drawing always seemed like so much fun but she never dreamed it could be a full-time job! She lives and works in a small town in England with her partner and a little black cat. When not at her desk she likes nothing more than to be outdoors in the sunshine with a hot cup of tea.

www.lucyflemingillustrations.com